The law was brought by Moses, but grace
and truth came by Jesus Christ.
(John 1:17 KJV)

THE LONG, LONG SHADOW

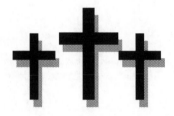

LaVerne Hutchison

abbott press®
A DIVISION OF WRITER'S DIGEST

The Long, Long Shadow

ISBN: 978-1-4582-0715-9 (sc)
ISBN: 978-1-4582-0714-2 (e)

Library of Congress Control Number: 2012922538

Abbott Press books may be ordered through booksellers or by contacting:

Abbott Press
1663 Liberty Drive
Bloomington, IN 47403
www.abbottpress.com
Phone: 1-866-697-5310

Printed in the United States of America

Abbott Press rev. date: 12/11/2012

This is the story of Mary, the Mother of Jesus. The facts for this story came straight from the pages of scripture. All Christians attribute Bethlehem to be the birthplace of our Lord. He was born of a virgin in the city of David.

In the beginning was the Word, and the Word was with God, and the Word was God. (John 1:1 NKJV)

The Word was made flesh, and dwelt among us. (John 1:14a KJV)

He came unto his own, and his own received him not. But as many as received him, to them gave he power to become the sons of God, even to them that believe on his name: Which were born, not of blood, nor of the will of the flesh, nor of the will of man, but of God. (John 1:11-13 KJV)

The first Adam is flesh. The Second Adam is Spirit. So we live by the flesh, and by the Spirit. When we walk through the watery grave of Baptism, we engage the Spirit.

Therefore the Lord himself shall give you a sign; Behold a virgin shall conceive, and bear a son, and shall call his name Immanuel.

(Isaiah 7:14 KJV)

CHAPTER 1

"NO! I AM NOT TAKING that child home with me. I never wanted her, and I'm not tying myself down with her."

"Well, you can't leave her here. I can't keep her."

"Then you can take her to the foundling home. I don't care what you do with her, but I'm not keeping her."

"Oh, yes, you are," said the grandmother, "you *are* taking that child home with you, and you *are* going to care for her in the manner she deserves to be cared for."

This conversation took place between baby Mary's mother and her grandmother, while her father paced the floor and she cried.

After the little family was home in their own abode, the father made arrangements for his sister to keep the baby.

"Can you keep our baby until she is out of the cradle?" he asked her. "My wife is going through a spell of melancholy."

"Ask Elizabeth if she minds, as she will be the one to do most of the work."

Elizabeth walked into the room at that moment and asked, "What's going on?"

Mannases turned to Elizabeth and said, "My wife isn't well, so we have put her to bed, but we need someone to care for our little one. She should be close to four months old now. Your mother suggested that I ask you."

"Yes, I'd love to care for her if I can keep her here. May I, Mother?"

"Be my guest. Of course. We will do what we can. I hope Hannah gets to feeling better soon. Do you think I should go to her?"

"In her present state of mind, rest and warm breezes is what she needs more than anything."

Mannases handed his little one to Elizabeth and asked what she wanted in the way of milk, for nourishment.

When the shadows rolled across the hill country, small Mary began a storm of crying. Her father had not yet left, having planned to help her get used to the new routine, but he was unfamiliar with all the crying and at a loss as to how to quiet the baby.

They took turns rocking and walking her, but to no avail. Then the auntie told Elizabeth to get out her harp. "Music may soothe her. It's as if she knows she is being cast aside."

As Mary lay in her crib, she slowed her crying, eventually quieting. It was as if she wanted to hear the music and realized that she couldn't listen and continued crying. This was her first awareness of her external surroundings.

The music became an evening ritual for the remainder of the year while Mary grew from a baby in arms to a toddler. On her first birthday, she was taken back to her mother, who was over her funk and who welcomed Mary into the family's home life.

CHAPTER 2

"**G**O TO YOUR ROOM, MARY. I see the rabbi heading in our direction, and that can mean only one thing." This from the mother of Mary, who was embarrassed at her daughter's being in the family way before the wedding had taken place.

"But Mother, I can't go on hiding! Everyone will know soon enough."

Hannah, flapping her hands, said, "Just go. Go! I can't deal with this right now."

Turning toward the door, Hannah met the rabbi with cheerfulness. "Why Rabbi, how nice of you to call, considering how busy you are kept."

"How are you, Hannah, and how about all of your family?" he asked as he helped himself to the wine that was always available so that guests knew they were welcome in Hannah's home.

"We are a family under duress, if you must know."

"I was afraid you might be, but she is lawfully promised to Joseph, is she not?"

"Yes, of course, that goes without question. But Mary claims he is not the father and that she has done nothing wrong."

"Oh? What else does Mary tell you?"

"She keeps insisting that she knows no man, and that God visited her one night."

"Y-e-e-e-s? Do tell me more."

"She said it was one night when she just could not get to sleep, so she finally arose to kneel by the window and watch the moon, which was high in the sky, but very bright. While she kneeled there, thinking thoughts of God and his creation, and wondering why the moon was constantly changing, suddenly God's voice started to converse with her."

"Did she tell you more?"

"Only that she agreed to become the mother of the promised one."

"I see … or maybe I see. Hannah, if what you tell me is not an image of the mind, this is momentous. You do understand the significance of what you just told me?"

"What? Pray tell!"

"It means that you must stop thinking of Mary as your baby daughter and start thinking of her as the mother of the Messiah—the promised one from our heavenly Father!"

"Mercy me, and may the Lord have mercy on us all. Oh me, oh my! Anything else?"

"Anything else? Isn't that enough, already?"

"I always knew Mary was a little different, but this is unthinkable." After a pause, Hannah continued, "What can I do? She refuses to change her story." The rabbi sat and pondered this for a few minutes while time moved quietly away from them. Finally he raised his head and reached out a comforting arm to Hannah.

"Is there someplace Mary can go into early confinement? We'll give her a little more time and then I'll question her later. Maybe by then she will be ready to tell us more. Does Joseph know about her?"

"Joseph is away, so he does not know! However, the whole village is abuzz."

"Lovely, lovely Mary. How my heart aches for you, my dear."

"It's sad, but who knows the heart of a woman. Look at me. I could have married you and had an orderly life, but no. I had to have Manassas. And even now, even when he stumbles home, my heart still calls out to him."

"I guess," the rabbi responded, "and I'm sorry for the hurt you have to carry for one of your own. Just be patient, and we will think of something to protect you and your daughters. And how are the other two taking it?"

"They are stunned into silence for once. I can't say that is a bad thing.

"If we could just get Mary to talk," Hannah continued, "it wouldn't be so bad, but she insists she knows no man, and we can be sure she hasn't been with Joseph because he has been on a journey with one of the caravans to get fresh supplies for the family shop."

"Give her time, but for safety's sake, can you find another place for her to go into early confinement?"

"Zacharias should be finishing his tour of duty at the temple soon. Maybe you could talk with him, find out whether he and his wife, Elizabeth, would welcome her into their custody."

"I'll do that. In the meantime, keep her safe the best way you know how. I'll be in touch, so keep your chin up."

"I never wanted that child from the beginning. She has been an embarrassment all along, claiming to see 'visitations' from the heavenly body and visions of the past, claiming to have been there to see it happen."

Hannah continued, "Sometimes I wish I had scuttled her when she was still a baby."

"Now, now! You mustn't have such thoughts. You know our God knows what He is about, and he never gives us difficulties he is not able to conquer."

"If you are sure, I'll try to believe it."

"Yes, Hannah, you do that. I'll have that talk with Mary later. Now I must be about other things."

CHAPTER 3

A s Joseph rode into the village with his caravan, men saluted him with exaggerated salutations all along the route to his family's carpentry shop. While he unloaded the materials, his partner surprised him by his remark.

"Joseph, you old fox, let me be the first to salute you, but how did you pull it off?"

"Did something momentous happen while I was away? I don't know what is going on."

His friend looked at him closely, took his hand, and looked directly into his face. Then his friend said, "I don't believe you do. Please let me be the one to inform you that your betrothed is in the family way, and the whole village is in a tizzy, being as how they missed out on the three days of revelry to celebrate your wedding."

Stunned into silence, Joseph took in the news. He turned

on his heel and fled to his home, where his mother met him at the door.

"Is it true?" Joseph asked. "Please tell me it isn't true."

"According to Hannah, it is true, but Mary claims the child is a spirit child, and she emphatically states that she knows no man."

"What do you think, mother of mine? With your unusual ability to identify deceit, what do you say?"

"I know it all sounds very strange, but for some uncanny reason, I think Mary must be telling her mother the truth. It is awfully hard for Hannah to accept, especially since she always guarded her daughters' purity as an old mother duck guards her ducklings."

"Then you think it is entirely possible, this spirit child thing?"

"We know the Father's promises, and who are we to laugh, as Sarah laughed, and took things into her own hands where Abraham and the angels were concerned?"

"Thanks, Ma-Ma, for your wisdom and guidance. I'll go to my room and pray about this. If what Mary says is true, I need to know, and if it isn't true, my heart is breaking. I do truly love that little girl-woman."

"Whatever you decide, do be gentle with Mary. She is very special to me, as well as to you."

"Yes, Mother. You know I will."

As Joseph agonized over the situation he found himself in, he washed himself. Toweling off, he said finally, "Lord, have mercy!" Then, throwing down the towel, he rolled onto his cot with a groan and fell asleep.

After several hours of uninterrupted sleep, Joseph was suddenly awakened by a loud roaring sound, as if a hard wind had suddenly blown the curtains down. He searched the room for damage, but none could be seen. It was then that one of God's heavenly creatures spoke to him.

"Joseph, the child that Mary carries is the promised Messiah. She tells the truth, and she needs you to protect her. Go to her, *now*. You will find her with Elizabeth in their mountain home. Do not hesitate. Mary is in need of a husband and the gentle care that only you can provide."

Before Joseph had time to ask questions and allow his doubts to interfere, the creature was gone, and he was alone again.

The prayer had been answered, so he arose and dressed for a short trip into the hill country. He called for a fresh donkey and was quickly on his way to see his beloved.

CHAPTER 4

JUST AS THE SUN WAS making its debut on the eastern horizon, Joseph arrived at the door of Zacharias and Elizabeth. He was lifting the latch to announce his arrival when suddenly the door was flung open wide, and there stood Mary, his intended.

No words were necessary. Joseph opened his arms, and she melted into his embrace. For a full five minutes they clung to one another in silence.

"You heard, then, what the villagers and our friends and family are saying," were Mary's only words.

"I've heard, but I want to know what you have to tell me."

"It was the Holy Spirit who visited me one night—a night much like this one. At least I think it was our Lord, or one of his messengers."

"Go on."

"He told me I would be highly favored if I would agree to

11

carry the promised Messiah. I was dumb with disbelief at first, thinking, *Who am I that our Lord would choose me?* But never once did I have any doubt about who my visitor was."

"I know, Mary. He visited me just tonight, and that is why I am here at this hour to claim my bride."

"Oh, Joseph, I'm so glad you came! I was beginning to wonder if I had been duped and had just imagined it all."

"May I come in? We need to talk to the priest and carry out many other things before we can consummate the marriage, but I'll make an effort to make amends for all the misery you have suffered.

"I'll take you to my mother's house. She loves you like the daughter she never had.

"I love you, too, Mary, and if you are with me in my mother's house, it should squelch much of the village gossip. Besides all that, I truly want to care for you and be your protector, like any other husband."

"Mmmm. It is so good to know you are back and that you are here."

"I think some of our family and friends are not so surprised at your being with child, because they think it is mine; but they feel that we deliberately cheated them out of a week of revelry. Remember, it isn't often that the prophet's niece and a son of David are betrothed!"

"It is something to think about, isn't it?"

"I don't want to doubt you, Mary, but I must hear it again from your own lips. Did you truly have a heavenly visitor? Did everything happen as I've been told?"

"I know, Joseph—it is hard to believe that a little nobody like me would be favored by the heavenly Father this way. Yes, Joseph it is true. I stake my life on it."

After a few moments of silence, Joseph finally responded, "It must be true, as strange as it all seems. Just look at Elizabeth. After all of these years of knowing she was barren, suddenly she presents the world with a son."

Mary added, "Not only that, but she told us that the heavenly visitor even told her what to name her little son."

"You are joking!"

"No, it is true. Zacharias didn't believe her, so he was struck dumb. We should all know better than to mess with our heavenly messengers."

"Tell me more. I was away and didn't hear about this."

"When Zacharias finished his turn at the temple, he went home to be with Elizabeth, and when she told him her good news, he was happy. But after all, he is our prophet and priest; he should know when it is the Lord speaking, and the Lord told both Elizabeth and the father to name the baby John.

"Zacharias made the mistake of disbelieving," Mary continued. "Then, just like that, no more talking."

"Is he still afflicted?"

"Not since he answered the call to name him John, and wrote it down for everyone to see."

"Strange things, they are happening."

"More than you think. It makes me wonder why John is so special, and if he is, what do we have to look forward to in another year?"

"Which reminds me of something: when is our baby due?"

"Oh, Joseph! How sweet! You can't begin to know how good it feels to know you approve of me. When I had my little talk with my heavenly visitor, I'm afraid I was so overwhelmed that I didn't think about all the complications that would follow after I said 'I'd be honored.' It was then I was told that I would be honored forever, in all generations."

"You will be, Mary. I'll do my part to see that you are." He continued to quiz her. "You need to answer my question, Mary, so we can make our plans. You know there is a census coming soon. I hope you will be able to make the trip with me, but if you are already in confinement, I'll do my best to take care of our duties."

"Oh! Let's see, Zacharias had finished his tour of duty at the temple, and Elizabeth was going into her sixth month. It was my heavenly visitor who told me that Elizabeth had conceived in her old age. That is one reason I left immediately to spend time with Elizabeth. Others may not be excited about our special news, but I knew Elizabeth would be, and we could glory in the wonder of it together."

"Has Elizabeth delivered yet?"

"The midwife has been here, so she must be due this week; I know our private time is over, so I was preparing to leave.

"Joseph." Mary was suddenly very shy. "I love you, and I'm so relieved to know you won't shame me before the entire village. I have worried some about the consequences, if people didn't believe me and thought I was a sinful woman."

"I love you, too, and even if what you told me hadn't been true, I couldn't let you be stoned. That would have hurt me as much as you."

"Why do you believe? My mother doesn't, and the people in the village don't."

"My mother believes you, and besides her assurance, the heavenly visitor came to me also. Much the same as the visitor Moses had. Only this time, it was the sound of a mighty wind, not fire, that got my attention."

"And so you are here, and oh, so welcome!"

While Joseph made arrangements for the coming trip to the home of their ancestor, David, Mary relaxed and learned the routine of her betrothed's family. As the time for departure drew near, Joseph's partner grew concerned about the traveling. Later, when Joseph had said nothing, the partner finally had to ask.

"Man, you are not planning to take the little woman with you on that hazardous trip, are you? Tell me you are not!"

"Let me ask you a question. Do you think she could be safe here, knowing how miffed her family and friends are?"

"You have a point there. I guess I wasn't thinking clearly."

And so it was that Mary accompanied Joseph and the others who were required to make the trip to their homeland to be counted in the census. It was not until the last night of the journey that Joseph told Mary the arrangements he had for them on arrival.

"If our baby decides to come while we are there, I don't want you to have to share a room with some rowdy individuals. Since I know the innkeeper, I called on him for a favor. You will have the peace and quiet of one of his stalls. There will be clean hay and bedding. There will also be a midwife on call, ready to help when your time comes."

"Oh, Joseph. You think of everything. How can I thank you enough?"

"Thank my mother. She is concerned for you. I might add that she is somewhat excited about becoming the grand-mère to the Messiah."

"She will be such a blessing in helping us understand all of this, and in getting him to adulthood."

CHAPTER 5

MARIANNE AWOKE WITH A START from a sound sleep at the inn. She sat up and rubbed her forehead with the back of her hand. She wasn't a midwife, and being present to watch Mary go through the pangs of birthing made her exhausted, as if she were the one doing it.

"My, what a night!" She spoke to herself, mostly, but the maid who was in the room with her answered.

"You ain't seen nothing, lady!"

"You mean there is something I missed?"

"Yes, ma'am. Just before dawn, the whole sky lit up as if the moon had turned to fire, and then those close enough got a taste of what the heavenly chorus sounds like when they sing in harmony and the bells ring and … oh, it was so wonderful!"

"And I missed all of that? I knew I was tired, but I didn't know how tired."

Marianne, the mother of Joseph, arose and prepared herself for the day before making the trip to the stable, where Mary and her baby boy snuggled into the sweet-smelling hay.

"Good morning, my dear. Are you all right? Please know that I'm here to be your slave for at least this first week. I'll do your bidding and be delighted to tend to our darling little one."

"Thank you, Mother … It sounds good to call you Mother."

"I understand that I missed the heavenly extravaganza in the night, and I am very disappointed. Did you see it?"

"Oh, yes!"

"Was it as grand as I have been told that it was?"

"Probably more than mere words can express."

"Actually, it was the heavenly Father letting the shepherds, who keep the temple sheep, know that their work during all of these generations has not been in vain. Now the real sacrificial lamb has been born." Mary continued, "It is hard for us to comprehend, but that is the way Zacharias explained it to me."

"Where is Zacharias now?"

"The shepherds came to see my newborn son, and he left with them."

"And I missed all of the mystery and beauty of this birth. It makes me sad."

"I know, Mother—it makes me sad, too. It was spectacular, almost as if the Father above was blowing his trumpet to announce the birth of a son."

"And that is exactly what he was doing. Isn't it exciting? I only wish I hadn't missed it all."

CHAPTER 6

A T THE END OF HER week in confinement, Mary looked up to see the priest Zacharias gazing at the sleeping baby. He saw Mary looking and asked, "Have you made plans for the ceremony of circumcision, or do you want that I should do it?"

"I've left everything in Joseph's capable hands, but I'm sure we will want you to do it for us."

"Is he here or anywhere near?"

"He left early this morning but promised to be back by midday."

When Joseph returned, he announced that he had arranged for his new family to move into a house in the town of Bethlehem.

"You can rest there until it is time for your temple cleansing,"

Joseph explained. "The trip back to Nazareth will be a hard one, so I want you to be fully rested and ready for the rigors of traveling with a baby."

"You are going to make an excellent husband and father, Joseph. You think of everything."

After the ritual circumcision, the little family, with Zachariah the priest, moved to the house with a grassy backyard. The household help had a light meal prepared, but Mary excused herself and found a place of solitude where she could rest and rock her baby son. She needed the rest, but she also preferred solitude when she felt the need to communicate with the heavenly Father.

A little later, when Zacharias went looking for Mary, he found her half asleep, humming to her tiny son, who was resting in the cradle of her arms.

He sat and watched for a few minutes, marveling at how mother and son seemed to be one package. He was once again amazed at how a mother seems to have a way of loving her child—one of God's mysteries.

Mary was startled awake when she realized she was not alone.

"I didn't mean to frighten you, Mary. I was thinking it was time to get back home and to my Elizabeth, unless you need more from me."

"I feel selfish asking, but it would mean a lot to me if you waited for the next group to go, so that when we go to the temple for my ritual cleansing, I won't feel so clumsy in not knowing which gate to enter and what to expect. Maybe you could pave the way for us?"

"I'd be glad to do it—you can count me in."

When the time arrived for Mary's trip to the temple in

Jerusalem, they left Bethlehem early, so as to arrive at the temple as the sun was peeking over the horizon. This was the time chosen by Zacharias. As they approached the temple, an elderly gentleman stepped out of the temple for a look at the show and to breathe in the dewy morning air.

When he recognized Zacharias, he reached for him and gave him a heartfelt greeting.

"What do we have here?" he asked with a broad sweep of his arm, indicating the little family.

"This is the cousin of Elizabeth and her husband, another Joseph."

"Would this babe be the one I heard the shepherds talking about so excitedly?"

"The very one. Please meet Mary, this one's mother. We are here for her cleansing ritual."

Simeon, the friend of Zacharias, greeted the two and then asked Mary, "May I?" as he reached for the little one. He carried the baby into the temple, and then, holding him high, he began talking in tongues to his Lord. He ended by saying, "Now I have seen your promised Salvation, Lord; and I give you thanks. This old man can die in peace now, knowing that you always keep every promise. You promised I wouldn't be called home before I could witness your glory. I came, I saw; now allow me to go in peace. Amen."

When he finished his prayer, a mystery woman appeared and reached for the little one. She held him to her bosom and repeated a prayer much as the one Simeon had prayed.

She added for the mother of the baby to hear, "This child will change the world as we know it. He will be both a blessing to all nations and spoken of as a curse on other lips. The evil one will pierce your heart, too, Little Mother. I think you should be forewarned."

She handed the baby back to Mary and said to her, "I have waited many years for this moment, praying always. Now I can die in peace because you have been gracious and shared this moment with us. May God the Father bless your name for all time. Gracious." She turned and left while wiping tears from her eyes.

CHAPTER 7

MARY WAS DELIGHTED WITH THE house Joseph had found for them in a nice residential area of Bethlehem. He explained to Mary and to his mother that it was near the workmen's shops. He thought he could probably find work in the carpenter's shop to pay for their living expenses.

"The pay is by the month," Joseph explained, "so it will not be as if we are purchasing the house."

The house was the center one of three that formed a U shape surrounding a grassy courtyard. Mary was so happy and so very content from the moment they moved into the furnished home. To her, it was home away from home. The child thrived in this environment.

One sunny day, as Mary's handmaiden busied herself with the many chores around the house, Mary decided to take Jesus to the courtyard, where he could play and she could visit with the close neighbors who were living and sharing the courtyard in their neat little compound.

Mary was happy, her child was growing, and everything was nearly perfect in her world. She stretched her arms to the sun and yawned, a very good feeling after the weeks of cool weather that had just passed. She took time to thank Jehovah for this great joy. At the same time, she wondered how long this arrangement could go on. Two years seemed to pass so fast. Could she dare to hope for another two years in this peaceful environment? She had an uneasy feeling of anticipation, as if the ax were about to fall.

Melinda was Mary's handmaiden and constant companion. When Melinda stepped into the courtyard entrance and gave a low whistle, Mary was so startled that she jumped.

"Is something wrong?" Mary asked.

"Something is happening on our street and in front of our house, but I don't know what it is."

When Jesus heard the whistle, which was a signal he recognized as a distress call, he joined his mother at the step. She took his hand, and the three of them entered the house together.

At the same time, the houseboy was ushering visitors into the house from the front entrance—strangers from another land.

Mary greeted them and asked, "Can I be of assistance to you?"

They all knelt suddenly before the trio, and their leader astonished them when he spoke. He said, "We have come to greet the King of the Jews. We have searched long and hard, but the star we were following led us here. Surely you will tell us we have come to the right place."

Because of her past experiences and her desire to protect her little son, Mary was very suspicious of these strangers. She knew Joseph to be adept at dealing with many different folks, and was glad to know he could be summoned at a moments notice.

Mary said, "Please allow me time to send for the child's father." Then she asked them to remove their outer garments and to be comfortable.

The houseboy heard her request and quickly ran to the carpenter's shop where Joseph worked. He motioned frantically for Joseph to come.

"What is it, Benji? Has something happened to Mary?"

"No, but she has called for you. You must come quickly!"

Joseph dropped the tools he was working with and raced through the streets like a madman.

When Joseph reached his street and saw the travelers' caravan, he tried, but to no avail, to figure out why travelers were in a residential area instead of at the carpenters' shops or at the unloading docks for any of the merchant shops.

Fortunately for all concerned, Joseph spoke fluently in all of the merchant languages. He walked in, greeted the men cordially, and asked what their errand was.

"We have come to bring gifts to the one who was born to be King of the Jews."

Joseph thought a moment and then spoke carefully. "You have found the right place. Meet our son. But please, tell me: how did you know?"

"We didn't. We had to take our chances."

Joseph was intrigued. He asked the household help, who stood about gaping and twisting their hands in excitement, to prepare a company meal and then sent the houseboy off to find fresh wine and water for washing. The travelers had obviously had a long and wearing journey.

He invited the strangers to a feast and said, "While we eat, you can tell us everything there is to tell."

For the time being, Joseph explained, "We stayed here in Bethlehem after the temple cleansing because we thought the excitement the birth caused would die down by now, and my bride and family could have a peaceful life here."

"We will talk later," said their spokesman as he was led away for the foot washing and clean garments necessary in order to be presentable for the family meal.

As everyone gathered together later for their prepared feast, Joseph bowed his head in prayer to ask for divine guidance for the guests and for his household, realizing for the first time, this visit from the magi must have been ordained by God.

"Now, sir," Joseph said to the spokesman. "Let's hear your story. How did you happen to come here to Bethlehem?"

"We didn't come here at first. We are astrologers of the first order, and we knew of the promise of a king for the house of Judah. Of course, we watched and studied the stars, wondering if it was time for the one who was assigned to be that king. When we spotted a new star, one we had never seen before, we became excited and studied it carefully for many months. When that star began to move like a bird across the sky, we were assured this was it."

"We are greatly humbled. Did you have a difficult trip, and did the star shine all the time, or did it disappear sometimes?"

"It moved slowly enough that we could follow. We rested when the sun outshone it, and we traveled by its light at night."

"We have always known the God of Israel helps his people,

and we knew of his promise of a Messiah who would rule Israel's people for all time. Therefore, we supposed the birth would be in Jerusalem, their special city. Naturally, we went there first. We talked with King Herod and asked where the new king was, but he acted befuddled."

"We explained to him about the promise of the prophets, and that we believed the time had come for the fulfillment. Afterward, King Herod called on his wise men to find out more about the prophecy. When he was told the prophecy would come to pass in Bethlehem, he relayed the information to us."

Joseph said, "King Herod has very little to do with the people he is king over, and that is such an irony. The people could rebel; it would not be hard, because we outnumber him by many. I think it worries the king and his court, and so he sometimes acts friendly and other times as though he hates all of us."

The quiet conversation continued well into the night. When Joseph offered to provide sleeping arrangements, he was told that was all taken care of by the city.

"We camp regularly when traveling," the spokesman explained, "so we have permission to make use of your town square."

"There goes our secret!" Joseph said with a sigh.

"Your secret?"

"We have been trying to keep this child's birth quiet to minimize the threats against him, but I guess the whole world knows by now."

"I'm sorry if we have caused you stress, but we know the God of Israel is a powerful God, and we want to be counted as friendly. To seal our friendship, we have come bearing gifts fit for a king!

"We brought gold because every king luxuriates in gold," he continued, and the gold was laid at the foot of the child's crib.

"And I came with frankincense for the nightly worship hour," said the second guest.

The third guests present Joseph with myrrh. "I thought it prudent to bring an ointment of myrrh to use when he gets the cuts and bruises active little boys are subject to getting."

Joseph was overwhelmed and left speechless after offering his gratitude; Mary went to her room and wept. She said to her Lord in prayer, "I can't believe this, Lord! How far have these men come to honor your king? It is all such a mystery to me."

Later, when Joseph joined her, they talked about all the strange occurrences. The sky was showing signs of the dawn before the two of them were able to fall asleep.

Joseph was shaken awake after a brief interlude of slumber. He heard a voice saying, "Joseph, oh, Joseph, awake. When your guests leave, you must be prepared to also leave. Take the young child and his mother. You will find solace in Egypt."

Joseph fell to his knees and waited for more, but no more came. By now he was becoming accustomed to these short and curt commands. He quietly arose and went to the shop to finish the project he had been working on the day before. As he put the finishing touches on the garden bench, the shop owner arrived.

"You are in a chipper mood this morning," Joseph greeted his friend. "Is there a special reason for your joy?"

"Only that the birds are singing, the rooster's crowing, and the sun is warm. Is all well with you?"

"I should be blissfully happy, but I'm sorry to say, my joy comes as a mixed bag."

"Does it have anything to do with your unexpected visitors from yesterday?"

"Exactly. Yesterday I received affirmation that my little son truly is Israel's long-awaited Messiah."

"And?"

"The downside is that now I need to leave you and this shop, which have kept me very happy for the last two years. I need to leave for parts unknown to keep the family safe. There will always be beggars willing to kill for a price, and I think King Herod has just put a price on our heads."

"I'm sure you have reason to believe that. How long do you have?"

"I'm here now to let you know and beg of you to act totally innocent of any knowledge of our whereabouts. It could involve you and yours, because who of us can trust King Herod and his men?"

"Enough said. Go, do what you have to do!"

"We will go toward Egypt, but no one needs to know."

"Amen!"

Joseph poked around Bethlehem, acting as if he had a job to do. He was listening to the local chatter and absorbing as much of it as he could, so that he could judge how safe their departure might be.

He heard quite a bit of talk about the caravan from the east as the people wondered what the travelers' errand was, and whether it involved their quiet little town of Bethlehem.

He listened but shrugged, as if he were as in the dark as they. He finally discovered from the blacksmith that a caravan was forming to head for Egypt at sundown. The idea was to travel by the cool of the night, and the group from the east would be traveling with them.

His burden of keeping Mary and her son safe had been lightened. By noon he was ready to go home to tell Mary of the necessity of leaving under cover of night. He worried that she might question the sanity of leaving, because she had become quite content with her little house, and in particular the household help. He was therefore relieved when she assented quietly and asked how much he thought she could pack to take with her. She then stated that her own maid would be going, because she truly relied on Melinda's help and companionship.

Joseph slept during the afternoon hours in preparation for the rigors of their flight to Egypt. As the time for their departure drew near, he lined up the household help to tell them of the plan. He instructed them to report to his boss at the carpentry shop and told them that his boss would find other employment for them.

Joseph warned them all that if anyone asked about him or Mary, they should say nothing: "It might bode well for you if no one knows that you have ever even known us."

"May I ask why, sir?" This from the houseboy.

"Because the visitors from yesterday warned us to flee from King Herod. We got word from them that our son is to be the next King of the Jews. You know the Romans can't stand the Jews, so now you know that to be safe, you must keep it to yourself."

"Yes, sir. Gracious, sir!"

CHAPTER 8

WHO COULD HAVE GUESSED JUST how angry King Herod was to become? When he couldn't find the little king, he ordered that all male babies under the age of two found in and around Bethlehem were to be destroyed. He gave the order for the soldiers to enter homes where it was necessary, and to make sure no male under the age of two remained.

It reminded the people in this quiet village of the Pharaoh's tyranny against the Jewish people who had lived in Egypt during his reign of terror. One grandfather was heard to sigh and say, "Will it never end? It just isn't fair!"

Mothers and nannies could be heard screaming from every household, it seemed, as the soldiers plunged their swords into sleeping babies or swung their heads against posts or outbuildings—all just to watch them die a gruesome death, and all because of the fear of God's appointed one.

No wonder the people began to wonder, "Who is in control—the God of the universe or the evil one?"

Joseph and his party had a full escort all the way into Egypt. As it turned out, the visitors from the east were returning to their homeland via Egypt and across the desert to the sea, to escape the volatile King Herod as well.

After the slaughter of the innocents, the little king remained alive. Such is the lot of the worldly when they act without knowledge.

The two years spent in Egypt were a lonely time for Mary. She was afraid to talk to people for fear she might let it slip that they were refugees from their homeland. Consequently she had time to ponder the welcome she and her child had received from the temple priest and especially from the prophet, Anna, the day of her visit to the temple. When Mary had doubts about her life, it helped to remember these blessings.

She also wondered why the heavenly Father had promised that she would find honor for all time. "All I have found is isolation," she said to her maid one day, as she sat in deep thought about all the drama and the secrecy being forced upon them.

Melinda, Mary's personal maid and companion, was a very happy young woman who exuded cheerfulness. As a native-born Egyptian, she knew her way around. Therefore, she could keep Mary informed of not only the local news, but news from afar.

Today when Mary complained, she said to her, "It won't be long now, Mary, and you will be on your way home again."

"What do you mean? You know something, don't you?"

"Yes, I was waiting for Joseph to speak, but he hasn't, so I hasten to tell you. The good news around the marketplace is that King Herod is dead."

With this, Mary plopped herself down on a nearby couch and blew breath across her face. She asked, "Is it true, my dear, or is it wishful thinking?"

"The word of his death was delivered by world travelers. I'm sure it's true."

"When we leave to go home, will you be going with us?"

"I was hoping you would ask. Yes, of course I will go."

"I'm glad," Mary responded, "because you are like a sister and a mother to me. I guess you know that my mother had a hard time dealing with me when I told her that I was expecting but that I didn't know a man."

"Don't hold it against her, Mary. I'm not sure very many mothers could have taken that without doubting. The people of Israel are known for the strange happenings among them, but some happenings are stranger than anyone can imagine. I'm not sure it is such a blessing to be called God's chosen ones!"

"We do get into some real pickles at times, don't we?" Mary thought about it awhile before adding, "And yet we cling to him as if he is our lifeline, which he really is. I'm not sure any of us could survive without him."

When Joseph arrived in time for the evening meal, Mary was there at the door to meet him. "Did you hear anything new today?" she asked.

"No, I can't think of anything."

Mary gave a sigh and said, "Tell me, Joseph, when will we be going home?"

He paused to wash his face, hands, and arms before he answered. He finally said, "You heard the scuttlebutt, then, about King Herod?"

"Yes, Joseph, and I'm wondering why you haven't mentioned it before this."

"Be patient, Mary. You must be patient. I have my reasons."

"Name one."

"All right, the main reason is this: When the Holy One awoke me to tell me I must hurry and get you and our son out of Bethlehem, he also told me to stay here until He called me. He hasn't called yet."

"Oh." All of the wind went out of Mary, and she wondered once again when her time of honor would come. Suffering seemed to attend all of her life. She didn't feel blessed as the Lord had promised she would be the night when every promise seemed so good.

"I'm sorry, Mary," Joseph said. "You have been such a trouper with all the inequities leveled upon you, but until the Lord speaks, we must not make a move. He has done so much to protect us, and it would not be prudent to doubt his goodness now."

"I'm trying, Joseph, I truly am. But all of a sudden I have an uncanny desire to be home, in our own community, and with those we know best."

"Would you be content to live in Nazareth? That is where I thought we could live in peace and comfort."

"Oh, yes, yes! I'm tired of this isolation. When can we leave?"

"As soon as I hear from the Lord. It won't be long, Mary. Your patience is appreciated, and I promise it won't be long now before we are on our way to Nazareth."

"Joseph?"

"Yes?"

"You said we can't leave until we hear from the Heavenly One. Does that mean we will be safe when we travel, or will we still need to move through the night like animals, scurrying through the high weeds and rocks?"

"I hope that won't be the way it is, but you heard about the slaughter of the innocents. It was only by the grace of our Father that we escaped. So, yes, and also no. I only know we are guardians of his own Son. Whatever is ahead, trust him. It is of utmost importance that we keep our guard up, but also to trust him the way you did the night you first encountered your heavenly visitor."

"I will try, Joseph. I truly will try. It seemed like a simple request then. I couldn't have imagined there would be so much to encounter."

"Do you have a lot of getting ready to do?"

"No, I plan to travel as sparingly as I can and yet provide for our household. I hope it won't be a long and difficult trip. Do you think it will be?"

"It won't be a bed of sheepskins, but on the other hand, we are not novices, so I think it should go well for us. Fortunately I know the merchant caravans well. They will keep us as safe as they can. We can thank our Lord for the experience I've had in the past."

"And I do. I thank my Father daily for you, Joseph."

With this confession of confidence, Joseph kissed Mary soundly and suggested they turn in for the night.

CHAPTER 9

A S THEIR CARAVAN APPROACHED JERUSALEM, Mary became anxious to see her sisters and her mother again. The closer it came, the more excited Mary became, so much so that she was surprised one day when her little son said to her, "Do you think they will like me?"

Mary was stunned into silence as she thought of a way to answer him. Then she said, "We are family, and family is supposed to love one another, so yes, I think you will be accepted. I know and can assure you that your aunties will like you instantly. As for your grand-mère, I'm not sure. That is the reason we will move on to Nazareth after we make our visit."

Following a brief and pleasant stay with Mary's mother, the family made their way to Nazareth. Here the little family grew and prospered. The other children were fond of Jesus. They laughed when he became frustrated with one of his projects, because when no one was watching, he could make do, as if he knew magic.

Jesus grew in wisdom, in knowledge, and in favor with God and man. He had his playtime, but more and more, he spent time with Joseph, learning the skills of a carpenter. This is where he shone and bonded with Joseph.

Joseph discovered quickly that when his shop had a rush job or an especially difficult one, he could assign it to his son Jesus, and it was not only finished quickly, but perfectly, with no apparent flaws.

As the two worked side by side, and Joseph observed the virtues of his son, he became more and more confident that this was indeed the spirit child his child bride had presented him with that cherished day so long ago—or at least it seemed like long ago, with all that had taken place. Was twelve years long, or was it short, in the scheme of things?

At this age, Jesus was allowed to make the yearly trek to the temple along with his parents and the villagers. While there, Jesus was in his glory as he discussed scholarly things with the scribes and Pharisees in the temple. He was so involved in the discussions that he forgot to count time.

His parents were well on their way home before they realized he was missing, and panic set in among their closest circle of friends and relatives. Jesus was totally oblivious until found and confronted by some irate parents.

Jesus answered saying, "Didn't you know that I must be about my Father's business?" (Luke 2:49b NKJV)

His answer to their scolding was proof positive to Joseph that this little son of Mary's was the promised one for all Israel.

With this knowledge, he felt more fully the burden of a father's position in a family.

Jesus grew to the age of majority living with his family in their villa. For the most part, he enjoyed the rhythm of life and laughter, though he was becoming increasingly anxious about his measured time upon this earth. While he patiently waited, he grew in wisdom and in favor with God and man.

While the family attended a family wedding, his mother surprised him. She had gone through the household looking for him, and when she found him, she frantically motioned for him to come near her.

"Mother, what is wrong? You look so worried."

"I am. Follow me."

She led him away from the guests, to the outer court, where the water jugs sat. She hoped they would be alone.

"Son, I'm okay, and you're okay, but there is something terribly wrong with the wine. Can you save my brother from embarrassment?"

"Mother, what has that to do with me? You know it is not yet my time?"

"Maybe it is. Who are we to decide?"

Mary turned to the servants who were present and told them to do whatever he told them, and to ask no questions or try to explain their own ineptitude.

Mary left and went back to the party. Jesus turned to the servants and said, "You all heard my mother, so here is what you must do. Fill every one of these water pots with fresh, cool water. See that they are full to the brim."

The servants knew they were in trouble, so they followed Jesus's command without comment. Some of them may have been disgruntled, but they worked without complaint.

As the revelry progressed, the guests naturally wandered from the house to the outer courts, at which time they were ready for refills to their wine cups. The captain of the wedding reached for the nearest water pot, wondering how he would get this exuberant crowd out the door with only water in their cups.

He had jerked forward and spilled a pint of the liquid on the stones when a noisy guest began to sing and to praise the quality of the wine. Soon all the guests were standing and pushing to get a sample of this most excellent wine. The party was over; the guests knew it, but left with a good feeling, one of praise and happiness.

Mary covered her panicked heart with both hands, and then she caressed Jesus's arm as she expressed her thanks to him. "You did well, my son, and I thank you."

"I'm thankful that you were the one chosen to be my mother. Turning the water into wine was an easy task, because I and the Father are one. Teaching this truth to men will be much harder, but it must be taught, because without me, there is no reaching the Father."

"Explain, please."

"I am the Word. I was present in the beginning, and I am the manifestation of the Word in the flesh. I was sent to dwell among men. I was sent to walk in men's footsteps, so the Father could redeem what was lost to him so many years ago. I am the redeemer."

"I understand, because I carried you in my womb even before Joseph and I consummated our love. But it seems so complicated—I wonder if others can believe it."

"Some will believe, and to those who do, there will be no death. The believers will transgress to a heavenly life, in much the same way that a fetus leaves the womb to become a newborn. Now you see what my Father's business is about, and why I must not while away more time doing the easy things of my existence."

"So go, my son, with my blessings."

CHAPTER 10

"THERE IS MUCH FOR YOU to understand, mother of mine. Our Father knew from the very foundation of the earth that there would come a day such as this. I wish with all my heart you didn't have to suffer along with me."

"What are you saying, my son?"

"You have known from the time of the announcement to the shepherds that I am to be the sacrificial lamb. The time will come, and now is upon us when every motive of every living creature will be questioned."

"And what has that to do with us?"

"From the very foundation of the earth, our Father had his plans for the redemption of man, and we—you and I—are the plan. The heart of man, even though he is made in the image of the Heavenly Father, is only flesh, and flesh is made with a deceitful heart. Even now one of my chosen followers has deceit in his heart. He will be known for all eternity as the man of perdition. But you, Mother, you will receive your rightful honor." Mary sighed at this revelation, and Jesus continued, "I have chosen a few men to be my companions, but after I am gone, the whole world will be turned on its head. You, my dear mother, must be a steadying force for my friends, because they are totally unprepared for the evil that will be unleashed upon this earth."

"Can you explain what and why?"

"Remember this: all things were made for your Lord's pleasure, even the evil, for the day of judgment."

"It seems as if there has been nothing but evil surrounding you from the very beginning," Mary mused. "If our Father above cared, you would think he could wave his magic wand and stop it."

"You mean as Moses did with Pharaoh?"

"Exactly!"

"But remember how rebellious and complaining the people were, even the ones who crossed the Red Sea on dry ground?"

"Yes, I see your point. Man's heart is a deceitful thing, and always will be—so where do we make any difference by our journey here on earth?" Mary was still wondering about every little thing.

"You have experienced the evil in the hearts of men and of women. Look at your own mother. She turned against you when you told her of me."

"Yes, how very sad that my own mother is counted with the unbelievers."

"You are beginning to understand. Many will be called, but few chosen to live the heavenly fever and to walk the golden streets."

The party was over, the guests had long gone, and the cool time of the night was approaching when Joseph poked his head around the corner to ask, "Is this a private conversation, or may I join you?"

"Come, Joseph," said Mary. "Our son is giving us some last-minute instructions and what to expect after the atonement. I do have that right, don't I?"

The three of them moved inside to a small sitting room to finish their discussion. Jesus continued explaining the events to follow. "When my time comes, those to suffer unduly will be my special friends, because they still think I'm going to become king and put the Romans under my command. They have not yet grasped the truth."

Joseph spoke up. "And the truth is?"

"As it has always been. Adam was the first Son of God, made in his image—but that is where the likeness stopped, because Adam lacked the Spirit of God. There are seven spirits of God, all of them good. Adam had but one of these spirits, so he begot children, but they were like Adam."

"And Cain rose up and slew his brother Abel," Joseph added.

"And it wasn't long after," Jesus continued, "that evil reigned. I am the atonement for much evil. Therefore, with much evil, there will be much suffering."

"Is this a warning to my Mary?" asked Joseph.

"Life won't change for the two of you, but it is my disciples for whom I am concerned."

"You mean it will be like in the beginning, when we needed to hide our identity?" asked Joseph.

"Somewhat like that, but my emissaries will take the brunt of the anger against the Father's plan, because it will be their responsibility to build my church. But the gates of hell shall not destroy it. Your responsibility is to be like a mother to them and to encourage and treasure them."

"I must warn you," Jesus continued, "after the resurrection, you will be traveling again—this time to a far country. After the turmoil, my people will no longer be safe in their homeland."

"You know a lot more than you are telling us, don't you?" Joseph asked.

"Yes, but I'm telling you the essentials for your own survival."

"You do understand, I hope, that when I said 'the Father and I are one,' I meant we are different parts of the same God, which is why I'm the one sent as the atonement for the sins of men. No one but me could have handled it."

"You talk as if it has already happened," Mary said.

"Strange talk, I know," Jesus answered.

"The hour is late," Mary said. "We must get some rest before we are overwhelmed completely with your last-minute instructions." Mary needed her own time to digest the latest request to once again travel to a far country. She knew she would do what was necessary, but she did not, and could not, look forward to it with happy anticipation.

CHAPTER 11

AFTER THE LONG WEEK OF the family wedding, everyone was eager to fall back into their routine of work and play.

Joseph went back to his shop, where he excelled in his carpentry work; he never tired of working with wood, bringing out its natural grain, and seeing it shine in all of its glory.

Jesus went to the temple to teach, where he amazed the Pharisees with his innate knowledge of the scriptures and of their application. When a few in the upper echelon became jealous of his ability to teach, they threw questions his way, intending to challenge him. However, he knew their frustration and took the time to answer each man and his question.

Jesus often mentioned the need to be about his Father's work, so when it came the lawyers' turn to challenge him, they made the mistake of asking, "What is our work, that we may attain eternal life?"

Jesus shot right back at them, straight from the hip, "Your work is to believe the One who sent me. The Father and I are one entity, so the one who believes me believes the Father who sent me—and when they believe, my Father claims them as his own children. Therefore, they cannot fail, because he will hold them and never let them go."

This was the method of teaching that took place each day as Jesus exchanged thoughts, and sometimes sharp words, with other men. It was a learning experience enjoyed by all who participated.

One day, as children played on the grassy knolls and women aired their homes while chatting leisurely with one another, the community was stunned into silence when John, the son of Zacharias, made a promenade through the city of Jerusalem in a chariot drawn by two black horses. He went directly to the temple and entered the gates as if the temple were his second home—which, of course, it was, because his father was famous for having lost his ability to speak until after this son, John, was born.

John's birth was one of those phenomena that folks didn't soon forget. The sight of the swift black steeds pulling up to the temple had them all on high alert, waiting for something unusual to happen.

One person said to another, "Isn't this the son of our priest? I heard that he was living in the desert and acting like a hermit. Some even say he acted as if he were losing his mind."

"That beautiful team and the way he entered the temple didn't exactly make him look demented."

"True, so I wonder what is afoot."

"It doesn't seem as though he is old enough for the priesthood, but surely he probably is, which explains his time in solitude. I wonder what it feels like to be alone in the desert."

"I would be scared spitless if I found myself isolated like that."

"I think it would be scarier to have been a David."

"Why, David, he had everything."

"Courage, most of all. Imagine being responsible for your father's sheep with only a slingshot for protection against predators who feast on sheep and young boys." This conversation continued for quite some time between two women as they idly revisited the past while waiting to know more about the young man they had seen disappear into the temple. Their curiosity was justified, for little did they know of the tragedies about to take place.

Chapter 12

JOHN WENT INTO THE TEMPLE to meet with the high priest. He was excited that he had finished his solitary time in good spirits and was eager for his oral exams.

The priest on duty asked him the required questions and received satisfactory answers. He congratulated John on his preparedness for the job of temple priest. As a final trial, he explained to John that times were changing, and as a final challenge, he wanted John to go to the River Jordan and preach his sermon there to the fish and the frogs.

The request seemed a bit unusual, but John accepted the challenge as one more lesson in being as effective a priest as his beloved father, Zacharias.

The next morning, at daybreak, John could be seen at the River Jordan. He moved over a large area of the Jordan, proclaiming what was in his heart. He had a good laugh when he stopped to think about fish and frogs. He imagined them standing at attention to his voice and then pictured the fish in men's attire.

Water carries sound, but he hadn't thought about that when he proclaimed words from the prophet Isaiah in his most solemn voice:

Prepare ye the way of the Lord,
make his paths straight.
Every valley shall be filled, and
every mountain and hill shall be brought low;
and the crooked shall be made straight,
and the rough ways shall be made smooth;
And all flesh shall see
the salvation of God. (Luke 3:4b-6 KJV)

When he stopped for breath, he looked up to see people coming to the river. It panicked him, so he sent up a quick prayer, hoping it would be answered. "Lord have mercy! What do I do now?"

In his panic, he lashed out at the people. He said, "O, you! Generation of vipers, who has warned you to flee from the wrath to come? Have you done anything lately that makes you worthy? You can't just claim worthiness by claiming Abraham as your father. Abraham has multitudes of children. Whole nations of children claim Abraham as Father."

"The ax is ready," John continued, "and any tree not bringing forth good fruit is ready to be cut down and thrown on the fire."

Then the people shouted, "What are we to do about it?"

His answer surprised them. "If you have two coats, give one to the person without a coat. And if you have meat, share with someone who is hungry."

Then came the tax collectors to the shores of the Jordan. They asked, "What about us? What do we need to do?"

John answered, "Exactly no more than is your due."

Next came the soldiers and they demanded that they count too, so what could they do to escape the wrath to come?

John answered, "First you must be content with your wages; discontent breeds discontent in the ranks. Do no violence for sake of violence, and for goodness' sake, do not make false accusations against your brother soldiers."

Next came one solitary man, walking by himself. He went to John as if he knew him, and all chatter stopped as folks strained to hear the conversation that took place between John and the stranger. Afterward, John turned to the people, who united expectantly.

John told them, "If you can repent of sins, I can baptize with water, but this man is mightier than I; he can baptize you with the Holy Ghost and with fire. He holds in his hand the fan that can blow the chaff away. The chaff he will burn with fire, the unquenchable fire."

When John realized folks were paying attention to his sermon, he became more impassioned in speaking about sins of destruction. He spoke of the sin of adultery and used Herod the tetrarch as an example. Herod was living in sin with his brother Philip's wife.

While John reached fever pitch with his sermon against the evils of adultery, somehow Jesus managed to wind his way toward him for the baptismal act of forgiveness. When John saw what Jesus intended to do, he became excited.

John stopped Jesus in his tracks and said, "Are you the one, or is there another coming?"

"I'm the one."

"Then I can't baptize you, because I have a much greater need to be baptized by you."

"No, that's not true. I need to do this here and now, while many are here to see and to hear. If I'm the example of godly living, I must show by example the need for baptism."

Jesus walked into the water for John to perform the act of baptism. When Jesus came back out of the water, the Holy Ghost descended in the form of a dove. This was beautiful and awe-inspiring, but when the voice of God was heard over the noise of the crowd as if it were filling the entire Jordan valley, everyone gasped, and the hush for a few moments was deafening.

The voice said, "You are My beloved Son; in You I am well pleased." (Luke 3:22b NKJV)

All the people heard it, and those who had recently been baptized were glad. They could now be counted among those saved from sin, not among the lost.

Public speakers and preachers are a special breed of people. Give them an attentive audience, and it is like saying "sic 'em" to a dog. John, the son of Zacharias, was no exception. After the baptism of Jesus, accompanied by the blessing of the Holy Spirit, the people strained to hear what else this novice priest had to say to them.

John spoke of the wrath to come. He told them to give up their evil habits and ask for the Lord's forgiveness. Then he explained in very descriptive words, which no one could misunderstand, just what personal sins needed to be forgiven.

Many people, young and old, were drawn to the riverbank to hear him, and many repented to have their sins washed away in the water of the Jordan. It became a major movement affecting all, throughout all of Jerusalem and beyond.

The ones who asked for forgiveness were touched by the

Spirit of God and did not want to return to their old way of life. The vast majority had given up on the promises of God and wondered why their God seemed so remote and uncaring while they were expected to keep up with all the religious ceremonies dictated by Moses and his appointed leaders. The heathens didn't follow any of these laws, after all, and they seemed to thrive.

After John told them a better life could be had, and that they truly were a special people and precious to their Lord; they all walked into the River Jordan as a group to ask the Lord's forgiveness. They vowed to do better and to rekindle their faith in God, and his promises made to them when they first had crossed the Jordan into the promised land. It seemed so long ago, but their elders still spoke of the trip and the many deaths that had occurred along the way. Now, as this new generation listened to the impassioned words of John, they could almost see it all unfold before their very faces.

Such a commotion of crying and whoops of happiness broke out that it caught the attention of the scribes and Pharisees, and even some of the Sadducees.

John gained a set of followers that day. They were happy that something was about to change—no more of the same dull ceremony of sacrificing the blood offerings. Perhaps some were beginning to understand the blood offerings and the reason for them.

To a great many more who heard of John's actions, all of that hope for change had seemed like a sham. Now that the young priest had chosen the Jordan River for his initial proclamations, even those skeptics thought something might be about to change. They could build their hope on John's promises.

The Sadducees continued to set themselves apart. No one

could ever convince such nonbelievers that life continues after physical death.

When Herod and Herodias, the woman Herod lived with in sin, heard John's sermon, the wife in particular became enraged. From the window of her palace apartment, she could see the fervor of the people and observe the baptisms taking place. Even some of her own attendants could be seen going into the waters of the Jordan. The longer she watched, the more riled she became.

Even though she knew the laws of Moses, this woman assumed they were there for others to follow. To her trusted handmaiden, she said, "That little upstart of a priest thinks he can get away with making an example of me."

Then she broke down in tears and had a good cry. No one wants to be called evil to their own faces; it was mortifying to this proud lady.

"He just doesn't understand my circumstances," the woman wept. "Surely the Lord of Heaven doesn't expect me to go on living with that self-indulgent dirtbag of a husband. He never loved me—he only wanted the chase. After we were married, he cast me aside and went looking for the next pretty lady to lay." She stopped to sob, and then continued, "This brother of Philip is a different man entirely. He treats me with respect and love."

Chapter 13

WHEN HEROD AND THE WIFE came together to discuss John's accusations, they formed a plan to make him pay for his boldness.

Herod confided to her that he was likewise offended and didn't want her to suffer any longer as an adulterous wife.

"Relax, my lady. I'll see that it doesn't happen a second time." And so it was that he sent word to his guards to arrest the man, to keep him quiet. "We will lock him away in prison and then see how many folks he can offend with his loose tongue."

Herodias was satisfied temporarily, but she still felt uneasy, because she knew that Herod did not fear John. In fact, she wasn't sure, but thought he liked John's preaching and would have secretly liked to have heard more. But this opinion was not shared by the women who were living adulterous lives, and certainly not by the wife of Philip and then of his brother.

With John the novice priest locked away, folks became somewhat disappointed. John had opened up the rhetoric and set tongues to work talking about sin as if it truly existed, and as if perhaps sin had consequences after all. The heads of households began to think more seriously about their responsibilities to their families.

While John languished in prison, the name of Jesus was heard more often, and soon John was forgotten, except by the few who remained acutely aware of their adulterous way of life. And so it was that the men of the village thought to confound Jesus. To put him to the test, they brought before him a woman they claimed to have caught in the very act of adultery. Jesus took one look at the frightened woman and had compassion for her.

Jesus looked at the men who stood gloating and then said, "Where did you find this woman?"

The gloating men knew by the question that they had exposed themselves as participants in the sin of adultery. They also knew that according to the laws of Moses, the sin of adultery was punishable by stoning—not just of the woman, but of both participants.

And so they quietly shielded their faces and slipped into the crowd in hopes of escaping their own guilt.

After the last of them left, Jesus said to the woman who stood before him, "Where did they go?"

"I don't know, sir."

"You mean you have no one to bring a charge against you?"

"It seems that way."

"You can be forgiven, and change your way of life; or you

can continue as you have been until someone bold comes along to bring you before the Sanhedrin for trial. Which will it be?"

"I would like to be forgiven. Are you a rabbi who can absolve sins?"

"You understand much, and yes, I can forgive. Go now, and sin no more."

The Pharisees, who were enraged by Jesus's claim that he could forgive sin, talked among themselves about how to best set a trap for him—an airtight trap, so he couldn't outsmart them and escape.

CHAPTER 14

THE ANGER AMONG THE PHARISEES and temple leaders was mounting. One day, as Jesus was teaching in the temple, they came for him, thinking he could be incarcerated. They thought wrong, because they did not and could not identify the man. So it was that Jesus slipped away in the crowd. The leaders knew his teachings and though they found the teachings, in many ways contrary to their own, they couldn't tell one Hebrew man from another, so it was easy for Jesus to get lost in the crowd. Jesus did not dress in priestly robes nor did he try to set himself apart.

Jesus often referred to himself as the son of man, so many followed him without realizing he was God Incarnate. They only cared about his power to heal the sick, the lame, the blind, and the possessed among them, so the crowds grew daily, always wanting something. They wanted either for themselves or for a friend or family member. They all seemed to be so needy, and with Jesus's great compassion, he found it difficult to turn away.

And so it went. Where Jesus went, the crowds followed. John the baptizer had spoken the truth concerning adultery and fornication, and it had cost him dearly. Jesus forgave sin and taught the people to love one another with empathy. Both he and John became the hated targets of those who could have gained the most from hearing the word of truth.

One day, as Jesus was alone with his disciples, he said to them, "The poor you will have with you always." He did not include the evil in that statement; however, he continued, "The prophet Isaiah spoke of evil when he told folks that all things were made for God's own pleasure—yes, even the evil, for the day of judgment."

Jesus identified himself to those who were eager to learn. He said to them, "I am the way, the truth, and the life. Those who worship me worship me in spirit and in truth."

Another day he told the crowd, "All those who believe in me and are baptized shall be saved."

It was human nature for his followers to want to know what they were to believe, and what they were to be saved from.

When the attorneys asked this question, Jesus explained they were to believe the one who had sent him to be their atonement for sin. The strange thing about many of Jesus's explanations though simple, they are at the same time difficult for many to understand. Jesus understands human error, the very reason he often called himself the son of man when in truth he was their Immanuel.

All the promises made by God and the prophets were meaningless when the people were afraid to recognize them.

For this reason, Jesus taught by inviting the children into the midst of his teachings.

One day, as the troops were entering a village, the crowds became so dense that Jesus found it necessary to stop where they were, to heal and to teach. When everything was quiet, the people would strain to hear, because they did not want to miss a single word that was spoken. They idolized Jesus and liked the way he taught, like no other before him. He taught them as if he could understand the intent of the laws, which had been designed to mean more than simply "Do this" and "Don't do that."

All of a sudden, a commotion erupted on one side of the crowd when some children tried to break into the midst of them to get to Jesus. The disciples of Jesus put up some resistance; they thought it was their duty to keep order in the crowd. When Jesus realized what the altercation was about, he stopped midsentence and called out, "Let them come; for of such as these is made the kingdom of heaven."

Then he took the little brother of one of those causing the ruckus. Jesus sat the little boy on his knee and continued his teaching. "Unless you have faith as that of a little child, you are not worthy of the kingdom of God. When you can receive me as that one whom the heavenly Father sent to represent him on earth, you are beginning to know what it means to have the faith. Sew it up with the baptism of the faithful, and it will be given to you as a gift. It becomes a part of you because you received it as a gift."

"How can that be?" the leaders asked.

"It is one of the mysteries of heaven. I say, repent of your sins, be baptized, and receive the gift of faith—a faith that will not let you down."

Someone in the crowd called out, "That's a lie—you are not God! How can you make such outlandish statements?"

Jesus turned his eyes on the skeptic and answered this way. "All those who believe and are baptized shall be saved. Those who do not believe are already condemned, because light came into the world to bring the light to the world, but men prefer darkness because their deeds are dark."

Then he turned to the child on his knee and he said, "Any man who would cause one of these little ones who believe in me to sin, it would be better for him if a millstone be hung around his neck, and he were drowned in the depth of the sea." (Matthew 18:6 NKJV)

This was such extreme teaching that it left the crowd speechless, as they thought about what they had just heard. The Pharisees in the crowd went away mumbling to one another.

CHAPTER 15

M ARY AND JOSEPH COULD ONLY shake their heads in wonder as they watched and listened to the chatter of their neighbors.

"When I said 'I'd be honored,' I knew in my heart there would be sacrifices," Mary said to her treasured mother-in-law. "You can't say yes to the Lord and escape a sacrifice or two. What I didn't expect was to see how people hang on his every word, and want more."

Marianne answered, "And have you also noticed how it irritates those who control what goes on at the temple?"

"After all we went through when he was a child? Yes, I've noticed, but he speaks with such authority that it is hard to worry about them."

"I just want to caution you to keep your distance, and let time and the Lord work their will into all of this."

Mary sat and studied Marianne for a spell and then she said, "What do you know that I am missing?"

"One day, when I was at the temple to bring an offering of thanks, I overheard two of the men there talking. They were behind a curtain, so I could take my time and eavesdrop in on the conversation."

"And what did you hear?"

"Their concern was about how this man Jesus was drawing such large crowds. It was concerning them because they were losing control—not just of the people's offerings but also of their teaching. Jesus has the people so off base, according to them, that their authority no longer seems to matter."

"Did you hear more?"

"I'm ashamed to say that, after hearing this much, I lit a candle and began a long prayer so I would have an excuse if anyone saw me there. And yes, I heard a lot more."

"Go on, tell me!"

"One or two men—I didn't recognize their voices, because they were talking secretively—but anyway, two, at least, were adamant. They wanted to call his bluff, to make him either deny that he had the authority to teach as he was teaching, or to lock him away as an imposter and false prophet."

"What else?"

"Two others, with cooler heads, said, 'Let him be. If he is not the one, the truth will come out, and if he is the Messiah we have waited for, perhaps we should put away our anger and listen to what he teaches."

"Did you hear more?"

"No, I left as quietly as I could. I had already heard more than was good for me."

Mary sat and pondered what Joseph's mother had revealed

to her. She loved her husband and also his mother. It bothered her that she had brought so much turmoil into their lives, yet she was so glad to have kind and loving people to confide in—especially in view of her own mother's rejection of not only her, but of the special son she had.

Now all she could think of was how complicated life had become since that long-ago time when the Holy Spirit had made his visit.

Mary's first impulse was to rush to her son's side and to warn him to escape to a far country, but then she recalled the night when she had had the encounter with the Spirit of God. This steadied her thoughts. Instead of acting, she knelt in prayer, hoping for another encounter that could indicate, without a doubt, whether to stay quiet and lost in the crowds or to be at his side. At last she decided to keep as quiet and as unobtrusive as possible. That was the only way she knew to protect her other loved ones.

"My, oh, my! Life does get complicated when we think we are on the path of righteousness," Mary said, more to herself than anyone.

At that instant, Joseph came into the room, and so he answered. "Have I missed something I should know about?"

Mary suddenly arose from her prayers to throw her arms about Joseph's neck and to hug him tight. "Oh, Joseph, I love you so much, and I'm afraid for you—and also our son."

"From all accounts, our son is doing a spectacular job of teaching and also healing the sick and the lame."

"Yes, that is the very problem: he is doing too good a job. It brings out the worst in his detractors."

Joseph raised his eyebrows in a questioning manner. Then

Mary said, "You need to go talk to your mother. Evil men are plotting against him again."

"I see. Well, that is to be expected, I guess. You do remember how we evaded King Herod's men when he was still a toddler? They didn't get to us then, but I'm quite sure the intents of the hearts of bad men never change."

"You speak as if you have been waiting all along for some evil to overcome us."

"Maybe in a way I have. If a tiny baby can stir up such irrational behavior, what can become of a new teacher—one who teaches as if his authority to teach is straight from God of heaven?"

Mary let out a little moan. She was weary of constantly not knowing how to protect and care for those she loved—and she loved them more than life itself, it seemed.

"Don't worry yourself, Mary. God will do what God has to do. Whatever we might decide to do can only be a distraction in the scheme of things."

"I know you are right, Joseph, so help me to stay in the background and keep my mouth shut."

"I'll try. I have a hunch our trials are just about to happen, so I'd advise you to pray for God's grace to be able to accept whatever comes."

"Wait, *have* you talked with your mother?"

"I don't need to; I heard a few things on my own. Don't forget that where I work, I hear most of the conversations of the common folk, and sometimes of the elders.

Joseph continued, "We have known from the time of his birth that he came for one purpose and one purpose only. He is the promised lamb without blemish, the final blood sacrifice as the atonement for all of mankind, if only they will accept that truth. No one can force another to believe it, but those who do will receive multiple other promises. Who are we to get in the way?" All of this was a lot to come from Joseph.

"I wish I understood it as well as you do, Joseph," Mary responded.

"You will, someday, and when you do, it will be easier for you to be still and allow the Lord's will to be done." Joseph rubbed Mary's arms to comfort her. Then he said, "Where there is much love, there is also much hatred. I'm sorry about that, but that is just the way the cookie crumbles."

"We all know the truth in what you say. I just hope I don't crumble also."

After this long conversation, Mary and Joseph, as well as their families, kept a low profile. They resigned themselves to just wait and see what unfolded where Jesus and the temple authorities were concerned.

CHAPTER 16

I N ANOTHER STRATUM OF THE society in Jerusalem, an elegant party was being planned. Herod's birthday was approaching, and his wife Herodias wanted to make it special. She wanted to show her appreciation to him for his part in chastising John for speaking so boldly about adultery, especially about adulterous wives.

Herodias had a daughter who was an erotic dancer. She knew how to use the many colors in her scarves to excite a man, so it was only natural for Herodias to ask her to be the final performing act at the lavish party.

All was ready, and the party was very grand. As the farewell act, the emcee for the banquet stood to make an announcement.

"We have enjoyed the company of all you good people. Now we have one special act for you to enjoy before we say good night. Please welcome our special lady as she performs her exciting dances for your pleasure."

When the lady had finished her dance, she left one of her silk scarves draped loosely around Herod's neck. The applause, catcalls, and whistles were deafening.

When a semblance of normalcy returned to the guests, Herod, to shower his favor on the dancer, asked what her price was.

"No price—I did it for my mother and because it is your birthday, and you are so good to my mother."

"I want to show my thanks. Name what you will have, even to half of my kingdom; it is yours to claim."

Salome, the dancer, deferred to her mother. "What do you want, Mother? After all, this is really your party."

"What do I want? I want John the Baptist's head on a silver platter! See if the man can deliver. I have my doubts, but we shall wait."

Salome went back to Herod to ask for John's head on a silver platter. Because of Herod's promise and Salome's request had been spoken out in the open, the king could hardly refuse the request without making a mockery of himself.

"You heard the request," he said to his attendants. "Call the guards and let the request be known, and be quick about it."

At last one of the guards approached the king with a charger covered with a linen napkin. He handed it to Herod and said, "Your name will go down in history as a name to scorn forevermore. Surely you know that this man, John, was a favorite of the people! They will not soon forget this act of cowardice."

Herod ducked his head in shame as he handed the

charger to Salome, who in turn carried it to her mother in her apartment.

The people were so incensed by the ignoble act that the family of Herod, Herodias, and even her daughter Salome were ostracized from that time forward. There were no more dancing engagements, and invitations for future events were either ignored as if they hadn't been received or regrets were sent in response to further parties. No RSVPs were received from those whom they had counted as friends.

They all learned that there are things that can be controlled, but no man can control the heart of another, certainly not when it comes to understanding right and wrong, as the people in Jerusalem surely did when they heard about the act. Even though Herod and his family were small-time elites, they soon learned what it meant to be scorned. It was then that the people were reminded of the prophets saying that vengeance belongs to the Lord. Any wrongdoing is his to avenge.

Many wept over the death of Zechariah's son, including Mary.

Life goes on for those who love, and for those who love not. It never changes, because human nature never changes. The only difference that can be visible to others is the changed life of one who becomes a believer and walks through the watery grave of baptism. In this act of obedience, they put away the old life of self-indulgence and take unto themselves the Holy Spirit. It can abide within, as does their own spirit, and it becomes their guiding light. The believer then can sing, "What a difference a day makes!"

Some of those who were baptized by John became bitter

after he was beheaded. They thought to themselves, *Nothing is different. Why did I believe what he was proclaiming?*

Others turned to Jesus in the hopes that he could help their unbelief. After all, John had said that even *he* was not worthy to unlatch Jesus's shoes. If John respected him so, there was surely more to this rabbi than met the eye.

Mary's maid and constant companion ran all these thoughts through her mind. Then, shaking her head, she wondered some more. *If I didn't know Mary, and know that she has no doubts … well, even Joseph claims he is special—a spirit child, he calls him.* Now, as for me, I can't help but wonder, *what if I had stayed in my home village and never heard the truth? Would the truth affect me? It's a puzzle. I know it's true by all the energy the enemy of the Jews expends to be rid of him. What about my families—are they exempt because they have no knowledge? How can anyone explain this to me? Is this a sign he is genuine? If he isn't, how can we know it? We aren't the elite and highly educated. We haven't had our own good sense educated out of us.*

And so it was that some of the disciples of John became disciples of Jesus, God's Holy Son.

It was an easy change, because the citizenry had been waiting a long time. But many decided the promise of a Messiah was a false report, and once their minds were turned against the message, they turned against the messenger as well.

In all of the confusion, Mary turned to Joseph and said, "This is our son, the one we love like our own foot, but it seems to me that he goes about deliberately antagonizing the very folks who are there to cause us harm."

She hid her face in Joseph's shoulder to cry silent tears. It hurt to the very core of her being to know that Elizabeth's special son had received such cruel treatment; if it had happened to John, what about Jesus?

Joseph was a man who truly cherished his wife; he wanted to protect her from the evils of the world. But at the same time, he was acutely aware of the unrest among the people. He had nothing to say to her to be of comfort; so he patted her on the shoulder, turned her about, and guided her in a slow walk toward their villa and quiet rest.

After much thought, he finally said, "We did our best to protect him long enough to get him to manhood. From now on, he is doing what seems right to him. It behooves us to stay away, to allow him to follow the course set for him. We have done what was ours to do; now it is in the Lord's hands."

ALONE WITH GOD

A HEAVY PALL HUNG OVER JERUSALEM and the surrounding territories following the crucifixion. The bone-chilling rain was so penetrating that men could not feel any warmth, even when standing next to a fire. The earthquake that had released some from their graves while taking others to their grave had added to the feeling of despair. No one could say whether this, too, would pass, or whether civilization had reached its zenith and there was no more future.

Joseph stood rubbing his hands for warmth and asked, "How is Mary? Can you see any change?"

"No, she only becomes weaker with each passing day," her maidservant answered.

"Is there nothing we can do to help her?"

"I don't know. She has gone so long without sleep. She tells me that every time she closes her eyes, she sees the agony on her son's face. Then she is wide awake again."

"Will she overcome it, or is the injustice of it all going to take her, too, poor thing? She has already suffered so much at the hands of those who are quick to judge and never ready to see their own folly."

Mary lay abed, twisting and turning until she was worn to a frazzle, but she still couldn't clear her mind of the recent events. She knew that her son had called on the heavenly Father to forgive those men who had been given the task of putting her son to death via the ugly cross. However, she found it impossible to be forgiving. Simply too many lies had been told, even before the trial itself. Not only were the witnesses bribed witnesses, which was against the law, but the trial was a farce in a make-believe court. How could anyone excuse such behavior—the impropriety of the trial, plus the beatings, and then the cross?

It replayed over and over and over in her mind until she was nearly crazy with anger. After many days, her constrained emotions finally could not be held any longer. Mary began to sob, quietly at first, but then more audibly as great sheets of tears wet her face, her gown, her bedding.

In her anguish, she moaned a prayer: "O Father above, hear my pain. Please tell me how it is possible for me, or anyone (except maybe you, O Father) to forgive the cruelty we witnessed the day your Son was killed. It was so awful, and yet he asked us to be forgiving. I'm sorry, Father, but unless You aid me, there is just now way I can forgive such treachery and abuse. How could it happen that way?"

Joseph, standing nearby, heard her cry out and came closer. Kneeling beside her, he said, "Mary, Mary, it isn't fair for the innocent to suffer at the hands of the ugly, but it has forever been that way. When our Father unleashed evil to let it have its way, we saw what happened. Now it is our turn to take up where your son left us, to let the world know there is a better way. One away from bitterness and defeat."

Joseph lay down beside Mary in order to take her in his arms to comfort her. He continued holding her and crooning softly long after she fell asleep from total exhaustion.

For twenty-four hours, Mary slept the sleep of the dead without stirring. When she awoke, her maid took her hand to pull her to a sitting position. "Good morning. Are you feeling better now?"

"Yes. I realize now that none of us can have the luxury of hiding away in our own little cubbyhole, for we must carry on with our Father's work. And thank you, Melinda, for being so patient with me."

"It was my privilege to be beholden to the little mother of her precious son. But what can we do now? Is this the end? Were we wrong to think he was the Messiah and would make injustice disappear?"

"No, my dear, not wrong. We just didn't understand. His work on this earth is finished, but ours has just begun. It falls to us and our children and our children's children to spread the word that my son was truly who he claimed to be: the Son of God and the Holy One who was sent to save the world from the evil one."

"Can you explain it so I can understand?"

"Later, when I can do it justice. Help me now to dress, for I must go to the upper room. Perhaps I can find something of his that was left—anything that I can hold or just smell. Then I'll know that this is not just a nightmare."

After a pause and in deep thought, Mary continued, "It

must be real. It has to be, because of the Father's promises at the time I conceived."

Mary turned her thoughts to her Lord. *I may not have acquiesced so eagerly had I any idea of the agony that accompanied the promises. You said I would be blessed among women for all time. I'm sorry, Lord, but all I can see is cursing and evil everywhere I look. What kind of blessing is that?*

Melinda's fingers were gentle as a baby's caress as she washed and plaited Mary's long and luxurious hair. She filled Mary in on a stranger's view of Jesus's death and the very strange happenings surrounding the death. Mary listened and pondered all these things in silence. When the Spirit had made his visit to tell her she would bear a special son, she had accepted it as strange, but true.

In anguish, she lashed out at the heavenly being who had made that visit. *If any of us can understand all this, please enlighten us. Was it really You who came that fateful night, or was it the evil one playing tricks? Please, Father, I need to know.*

While Mary bathed, the heavenly Father came to her. She heard His voice as she sat brooding.

"Mary, Mary. You must know that I have loved ones who are not of this fold. What I do, I do for all of mankind. Some will come when chosen, and others will reject the call, but they must have their call. And, yes, you will be blessed by those of whom you know not."

Mary had much to ponder with the heavenly Father while the handmaiden became impatient with what she thought to be dawdling.

Mary took time to eat a piece of dry bread with cheese, and sipped a little red wine to replenish her energy. Then she and

Melinda slowly made their way to the upper room of the family villa. Melinda stood in the doorway to allow Mary the solitude she so dearly sought.

Mary walked the full length of the room and leaned briefly on the chair at the end of the table. She moved around the table and, seeing a stool that had been pushed against the wall, she sat to rest. Suddenly, her eyes lit up as she saw the shine of the tin cup that had held the wine her son had sipped. She reached for it and pressed it to her lips.

"At least I'll have this to keep as a memento."

The news of Mary's stirrings spread through the villa quickly, and others began arriving in the upper room. When Mary saw them, she handed the cup to Melinda for safekeeping.

"Keep this safe, and from other hands, please. I haven't much left, but I will keep the cup."

Joseph of Arimathea, whose title was on the villa where the family resided, had been out and about on horseback. He had many businesses to see about before his return to the Isles of the Sea and his tin mines. He was very concerned for his little niece, but felt that it was better for him to stay away. That way she could have some semblance of privacy for her grieving.

When a courier reached him with the message that Mary had slept, he was greatly relieved. In a moment's time, he decided it would be unsafe to leave Mary in Jerusalem, where the unrest was at fever pitch. He galloped back to the villa to see Mary and the little group gathered there. He was greatly surprised when he found they were all of one accord gathered in the upper room.

"Has something more happened?" he asked. "What is going on?"

"Oh, Joseph! You should have been here!"

"Why?"

"You just missed him. He isn't dead at all. He was here!"

"How can you say such things? I know He's dead. I took him to the grave and saw that it was sealed tight."

"No! No! It was Him. He talked to us and showed us His wounds where the nails had pierced His hands."

Joseph looked at Mary to see how she was taking all of this scuttlebutt. When he saw a divine glow underneath the haggard expression, he licked his lips and suddenly sat down to keep from staggering.

"Tell me more," he said.

"We were all here, because we saw Mary come this way, and we wanted to be where she was," someone said. Then they all fell silent and waited for the handmaiden of Mary to continue.

"Mary picked up the wine cup from the Passover Feast and rubbed it where she saw a lip smudge," Melinda explained, "and when she did that, we all heard a sound like a mighty wind. We looked toward the door, but everything was quiet. And then, in the dark corner of the room, just as if someone had lit a lamp, all of a sudden there He stood. Just like a beacon of light."

"Is this true what I've been told?" Joseph of Arimathea asked.

Each one standing there nodded affirmatively, in awe and in reverence.

"I think you know what this means, don't you?"

"What?" they asked.

"It means he truly is the Christ, the Holy One of the Most High God."

Silence followed Joseph's statement followed by an audible "whoosh" as they all let their breath out in unison.

Then Joseph continued as the one who was in the habit of giving commands and bringing order from chaos.

"I want each of you to go quietly, so as not to pique curiosity, but do the necessary things to prepare to set sail as quickly as possible. Melinda, you prepare Mary and her household for a long journey by boat."

He turned to his steward and said, "You do the usual to prepare for my trip to the Isles, but expand it to include this household. We must go quickly and quietly, or we may be detained by those who wanted Jesus out of their way.

"Do all of you understand the situation?"

"We do."

"Then make haste. We meet here in twenty-four hours, prepared for a long journey. If there be any one of you who wants to stay, let us hear from you now."

Only one man spoke. "I'm too old and too feeble to make a trip like that, so I'll stay here and tend the home fires. By the time the daylight comes the second day, you should be well on your way."

"Is everyone agreed?" Everyone was. "Go, then. Each to their own task."

What to take and what to leave, or maybe put into storage, was utmost in the thoughts of this small band of followers and friends of Jesus. Each in their own way knew that he or she was bidding farewell to this home forever. To have but twenty-four hours to make major decisions turned into a blessing in disguise.

They all thought they would be leaving in a large ship. However, the man in charge decided that a half dozen smaller boats leaving at intervals would be less noticeable. And so it was that at dusk, when there was a natural migration of people and animals, the last of the little band stepped outside the villa for the final time.

Joseph of Arimathea directed each band and gave the signal when it was time for each to move along toward the boat dock. Six groups of six went quietly with the appointed leader, but by the time Joseph, Mary, and the husband of Mary were ready to leave, a Roman soldier rode by in all his finery. When he recognized the group as those he had seen at the grave of the crucified one, he did an abrupt turn and came back to where the trio stood. He stared at them as if he had been left speechless.

Finally, he spoke. "And where might you be going on a fair night like this?"

He rode back and forth in front of them, as if wondering what, if anything, he should do about this trio.

"Tell me," he said to Joseph of Arimathea, "aren't you the rich man, the man of many tin mines? Why would you need to be out with these nondescript people at such an hour?"

"You are right as to my identification, and don't you know that a man with irons to burn cannot be away from his business for any length of time? I go to my ship now, while the sea is calm, so that I won't find myself leaving in a storm."

"Come, allow me and my man here to escort you then, to see you on your way."

When they arrived at the dock, the captain looked for a ship, and when he saw there was only a small vessel, he became suspicious and challenged Joseph.

"Please don't tell me that a man of your means is leaving in a fisherman's craft and in the night. You must take me for the village idiot!"

"Believe me, we have a larger ship arranged for traveling. It is in deeper water—hence the necessity for this small boat."

The horseman ushered them aboard without further comment, then picked up the oars and took them ashore.

"With the gorgeous night and the bright moon, you won't need these, I gather, so I'll just take them with me." This he said with a sardonic smile.

As the little group watched the soldier disappear from sight, they stood feeling completely bereft of love. Finally, Mary spoke. She turned toward the two Josephs and said, "Well, if our God wants us to live, and to carry on with my son's work, we should ask for His guidance."

She kneeled to pray, and the two men followed suit. While they prayed, Bartholomew, the apostle and close friend of Jesus, suddenly came quietly alongside them in his boat. Without a word, he beckoned for them to join him.

Mary's valise was tossed to Bartholomew, and then Mary followed, with the men steadying her as she made her way from one vessel to the other. The two Josephs glided into the water, and then, with one on either side of the boat to balance it, they found it easy to get aboard. This entire exercise took place in total silence, because by now, they had been made to feel as if they were criminals making a break for freedom. They were also wise in the ways of the water and knew that on a quiet night like tonight, sound could carry for a mile or more, and be as clear as a bell ringing next door. They left their personal possessions and the food in the deserted craft. If it were found with the personal items intact, it would give the finder the idea that the escapees had drowned.

After the week of rain and damp drizzle of Jerusalem, the travelers welcomed the peace of the sea. A white moon overhead lit their way just enough to enable them to reach the fisherman's village with no trouble. The ship that was to take them to the

Isles, where the tin mines were located, was anchored in deeper waters, just as Joseph had said.

"Our first stop will be in Gaul, where the weary can rest—especially our Mary. She has had no rest during this last ordeal as the mother of our Lord. While you folks rest, I have some merchants and artisans I need to see.

"So I want you all to rest and enjoy the sunny port in the south of Gaul," he continued. "When we get to the Isles, where my business is headquartered, you may not find the sun for a while. Tonight we spend here with friends. Tomorrow at daybreak, we get under way."

When their small vessel pulled ashore where they expected to meet the others, they were surprised to see someone already had a fire burning and fish prepared for them to eat.

It made Mary gasp; she thought she was seeing double. She rubbed her eyes, shook her head, and then took a second look. *Yes,* she thought, *this is my son.* And: *No, surely, I'm not losing my mind. I know he told us he was God Incarnate. It must be that I am finally, after all of this time, beginning to comprehend. Forgive me, Lord. I'm so slow to get it.*

Even with all that happened when he was only a babe and growing up, I didn't understand. Now, I get it! Lord, help me to be worthy of such a trust. I didn't deserve it. I complained, I pouted, I felt sorry for myself. Now I feel totally overwhelmed. Amen.

After a short pause, she continued: *I carried you in my womb, and even then I was so naive; I did not comprehend that it was you all along, dressed in human flesh!*

Forgive me, Father. Keep me protected and alive for as long as it takes for me to make up for being so ignorant! Amen, amen, and amen.

Mary thought awhile and then continued her prayer. *All*

of this time I thought of Jesus as my son, even though you call him Your Son, and he likes to refer to himself as the Son of Man. Suddenly I see as clearly as if I had looked in a mirror. Our Son, yours and mine, is the promised Messiah. Therefore, we are all right, because he is the Word all dressed up in human flesh.

Our Emanuel!

Hallelujah!

Even though Mary had caught a glimpse of her son while they were in the upper room and knew that he had returned from the dead, just as he had told them he would, it was humbling to see that it had actually happened.

Anyone who gets a glimpse of the heavenly is awestruck, and Mary was no different. His appearance in bodily form helped her, and those with her, to comprehend the disbeliefs of others, and it helped Mary to understand and to forgive her own mother.

When Mary and the two Josephs came ashore, Jesus was already in a deep and singular discussion with Peter and those with him. Mary went to seek her maid, who had arrived in one of the first boats to leave the shores of the Mediterranean Lake.

After finding the maid, Mary settled down beside her to listen to this serious discourse. As she listened, she became almost panicked about the size of the task that lay ahead of them, for she heard her son telling Peter this, well within earshot of those who were with him: "You know, Simon, when first I met you, I changed your name to Peter, meaning 'the rock.'"

"Yes, I remember that day and how I wondered about it."

"Here is your answer. When I died, the heavenly Father simultaneously tore the curtain dividing the temple from the Holy of Holies. The tearing of the temple curtain brought finesse to the worship with bulls and goats. I was the one great sacrifice, made for all humanity and for all time.

"Remember this: People, even my chosen ones, have a hard time believing there could be a virgin birth. Add the idea of returning from the grave, and folks find it even harder to believe."

"I think we understand their unbelief," Peter responded, "but what does it have to do with me and the other disciples?"

"I called you 'the rock' because you are to be the doorstep, the cornerstone, the East Gate of the church and the worshippers who follow after I ascend to heaven.

"I need to know you won't break underneath the load I'm leaving you with, and so I'll ask one more time. Simon, do you love me?"

"You know I do, Lord."

"I don't mean superficially. I mean enough to lay down your life when the way turns ugly."

"Yes, Lord. I intend to remain steady."

"When the big boys come for you to hang you on that ugly cross, what will you do then?"

"I love you, Lord, but I know that love is not worthy of the same cross that took your life. No, I couldn't go the same way. I should ask to be hung with my head toward the ground."

Jesus took Peter's shoulders between his two hands and turned him to face the little group gathered by the fire that quiet night.

"This, dear ones, is my rock. Please know that it is upon this rock that I build my church. I'll never leave him, nor forsake him. What he decides in any controversy stands, and what he allows to stand stands. Do you understand?"

While the men stood talking, a cloud descended from

heaven to encompass Jesus. It slowly lifted him from the ground into heaven. After even his shadow disappeared, the men stood gazing into heaven where Jesus and been.

Finally someone was heard to say, "Why do you men stand here, gazing into heaven?"

To this group of believers, seeing Jesus ascend to heaven was in some ways more grief than the day they laid him in the grave. John layed his hand on Peter's shoulder to draw some comfort and to also give a little comfort. He then said to Peter, "He is gone. No one but the heavenly Father knows when his return will be—no, not even Jesus the Son. It is in your hands now, Peter. If you fail, an entire generation fails, and our Lord gave up his life for nothing. This is why you heard him say before he ascended to heaven, 'Upon this rock I will build my church.'"

Hail Mary, Mother of God. Blessed art thou among women, and blessed is the fruit of thy womb.

He was born in Bethlehem of Judea.

He called his son out of Egypt.

He was called a Nazarene.